**DATE DUE**

THE CHILD'S WORLD®

# The Tale of Mrs. Tittlemouse

*Written by Beatrix Potter • Illustrated by Wendy Rasmussen*

*For Timothy and Grace*

Published in the United States of America by The Child's World®
1980 Lookout Drive • Mankato, MN 56003-1705
800-599-READ • www.childsworld.com

ACKNOWLEDGMENTS
The Child's World®: Mary Berendes, Publishing Director
Editorial Directions, Inc.: E. Russell Primm, Editor; Dina Rubin, Proofreader
The Design Lab: Kathleen Petelinsek, Design; Victoria Stanley, Production Assistant

TEXT

ILLUSTRATIONS
© 2010 by Wendy Rasmussen

LIBRARY OF CONGRESS CATALOGING-IN-PUBLICATION DATA
Potter, Beatrix, 1866–1943.
  The tale of Mrs. Tittlemouse / by Beatrix Potter ; illustrated by Wendy Rasmussen.
    p. cm. — (Classic tales)
  Summary: The story of a little mouse's funny house, the visitors she has there, and
how she finally rids herself of the untidy, messy ones.
  ISBN 978-1-60253-294-6 (library bound : alk. paper)
  [1. Mice—Fiction.] I. Rasmussen, Wendy, 1952– ill. II. Title. III. Series.
PZ7.P85Tal 2009
  [E]—dc22                              2009001635

# The Tale
# of Mrs.
# Tittlemouse

nce upon a time, there was a wood mouse, and her name was Mrs. Tittlemouse.

She lived in a bank under a hedge.

Such a funny house! There were yards and yards of sandy passages, leading to storerooms and nut cellars and seed cellars, all among the roots of the hedge.

There was a kitchen, a parlor, a pantry, and a larder.

Also, there was Mrs. Tittlemouse's bedroom, where she slept in a little box bed!

Mrs. Tittlemouse was a most terribly tidy, particular little mouse, always sweeping and dusting the soft sandy floors.

Sometimes, a beetle lost its way in the passages.

"Shuh! Shuh! Little dirty feet!" said Mrs. Tittlemouse, clattering her dustpan.

And one day a little old woman ran up and down in a red spotty coat.

"Your house is on fire, Mother Ladybird! Fly away home to your children!"

Another day, a big fat spider came in to shelter from the rain.

"Beg pardon, is this not Miss Muffet's?"

"Go away, you bold bad spider! Leaving ends of cobweb all over my nice clean house!"

She bundled the spider out at a window.

He let himself down the hedge with a long thin bit of string.

Mrs. Tittlemouse went on her way to a distant storeroom, to fetch cherry-stones and thistledown seed for dinner.

All along the passage she sniffed and looked at the floor.

"I smell a smell of honey. Is it the cowslips outside, in the hedge? I am sure I can see the marks of little dirty feet."

Suddenly, around a corner, she met Babbitty Bumble. "*Zizz, bizz, bizzz!*" said the bumblebee.

Mrs. Tittlemouse looked at her
severely. She wished that she had a broom.
"Good day, Babbitty Bumble. I
should be glad to buy some beeswax. But
what are you doing down here? Why do
you always come in at a window, and
say *zizz, bizz, bizzz?*" Mrs. Tittlemouse
began to get cross.

"*Zizz, wizz, wizzz!*" replied Babbitty Bumble in an irritable squeak. She moved sideways down a passage and disappeared into a storeroom, which had been used for acorns.

Mrs. Tittlemouse had eaten the acorns before Christmas. The storeroom ought to have been empty.

But it was full of untidy dry moss.

Mrs. Tittlemouse began to pull out the moss. Three or four other bees put their heads out and buzzed fiercely.

"I am not in the habit of letting lodgings. This is an intrusion!" said Mrs. Tittlemouse. "I will have them turned out."

"*Buzz, buzz, buzzz!*"

"I wonder who would help me?"

"*Bizz, wizz, wizzz!*"

"I will not have Mr. Jackson. He never wipes his feet."

Mrs. Tittlemouse decided to leave the bees till after dinner.

When she got back to the parlor, she
heard someone coughing in a fat voice,
and there sat Mr. Jackson himself!

He was sitting all over a small rocking
chair, twiddling his thumbs and smiling,
with his feet on the railing.

He lived in a drain below the hedge,
in a very dirty wet ditch.

"How do you do, Mr. Jackson? Deary
me, you have gotten very wet!"

"Thank you, thank you, thank you, Mrs. Tittlemouse! I'll sit awhile and dry myself," said Mr. Jackson.

He sat and smiled, and the water dripped off his coattails. Mrs. Tittlemouse went around with a mop.

He sat such a while that he had to be asked if he would take some dinner.

First she offered him cherry-stones. "Thank you, thank you, Mrs. Tittlemouse! No teeth, no teeth, no teeth!" said Mr. Jackson.

He opened his mouth most unnecessarily wide. He certainly had not a tooth in his head.

Then she offered him thistledown seed. "*Tiddly, widdly, widdly! Pouff, pouff, puff!*" said Mr. Jackson. He blew the thistledown all over the room.

"Thank you, thank you, thank you, Mrs. Tittlemouse! Now what I really— *really* should like—would be a little dish of honey!"

"I am afraid I have not got any, Mr. Jackson," said Mrs. Tittlemouse.

"*Tiddly, widdly, widdly,* Mrs. Tittlemouse!" said the smiling Mr. Jackson. "I can *smell* it. That is why I came to call."

Mr. Jackson rose clumsily from the table and began to look into the cupboards.

Mrs. Tittlemouse followed him with a dishcloth, to wipe his large wet footmarks off the parlor floor.

When he had convinced himself that there was no honey in the cupboards, he began to walk down the passage.

"Indeed, indeed, you will stick fast, Mr. Jackson!"

"*Tiddly, widdly, widdly,* Mrs. Tittlemouse!"

First he squeezed into the pantry.

"*Tiddly, widdly, widdly*? No honey? No honey, Mrs. Tittlemouse?"

There were three creepy-crawly people hiding in the plate rack. Two of them got away, but the littlest one he caught.

Then he squeezed into the larder. Miss Butterfly was tasting the sugar, but she flew away out of the window.

"*Tiddly, widdly, widdly,* Mrs. Tittlemouse, you seem to have plenty of visitors!"

"And without any invitation!" said Mrs. Thomasina Tittlemouse.

They went along the sandy passage.

"*Tiddly, widdly.*"

"*Buzz, wizz, wizz!*"

He met Babbitty around a corner, snapped her up, and put her down again.

"I do not like bumblebees. They are all over bristles," said Mr. Jackson, wiping his mouth with his coat sleeve.

"Get out, you nasty old toad!" shrieked Babbitty Bumble.

"I shall go distracted!" scolded Mrs. Tittlemouse.

She shut herself up in the nut cellar while Mr. Jackson pulled out the bees nest. He seemed to have no objection to stings.

When Mrs. Tittlemouse ventured to come out, everybody had gone away.

But the untidiness was something

dreadful. "Never did I see such a mess—
smears of honey, moss, and thistledown
and marks of big and little dirty feet—all
over my nice clean house!"

She gathered up the moss and the
remains of the beeswax.

Then she went out and fetched some
twigs, to partly close up the front door.

"I will make it too small for Mr.
Jackson!"

She fetched soft soap, a soft cloth,
and a new scrubbing brush from the
storeroom. But she was too tired to do
any more. First she fell asleep in her chair,
and then she went to bed.

"Will it ever be tidy again?" said poor
Mrs. Tittlemouse.

Next morning, she got up very early
and began a spring-cleaning that lasted
for two weeks.

She swept, scrubbed, and dusted, and she rubbed up the furniture with beeswax and polished her little tin spoons.

When it was all beautifully neat and clean, she gave a party to five other little mice, without Mr. Jackson.

He smelled the party and came up the bank, but he could not squeeze in at the door.

So they handed him out acorn-cupfuls of honeydew through the window, and he was not at all offended.

He sat outside in the sun and said, "*Tiddly, widdly, widdly!* Your very good health, Mrs. Tittlemouse!"

## ABOUT BEATRIX POTTER

When Beatrix Potter (1866–1943) was growing up in England, she did not go to a regular school. Instead, she stayed at home and was educated by a governess. Beatrix didn't have many playmates, other than her brother, but she had numerous pets, including birds, mice, lizards, and snakes. She enjoyed drawing her pets, and they later served as inspiration for her books.

As a young girl, Beatrix enjoyed going for walks in the country. She began drawing the animals and plants she saw. For several years, she also kept a secret journal, written in her own special code. The journal's code was not understood until after Beatrix died.

In 1893, when Potter was twenty-seven years old, she wrote a story for a little boy who was sick. That story became *The Tale of Peter Rabbit*. In 1902, the book was published and featured illustrations drawn by Potter herself. Her next book was *The Tale of Squirrel Nutkin*, which was published in 1903. Potter went on to write twenty-three books, all that were easy for children to read.

When Potter was in her forties, she bought a place called Hill Top Farm in England. She began breeding sheep and became a respected farmer. She was concerned about the farmland and preserving natural places. When she died, Potter left all of her property, about 4,000 acres (1,600 hectares), to England's National Trust. This land is now part of the Lake District National Park. Today, the National Trust manages the Beatrix Potter Gallery, which displays her original book illustrations.

## About Wendy Rasmussen

Drawing from the time she could hold her first crayon, Wendy Rasmussen grew up on a farm in southern New Jersey surrounded by the animals and things that often appear in her work. Rasmussen studied both biology and art in college. Today she illustrates children's books, as well as medical and natural-science books.

Today, Rasmussen lives in Bucks County, Pennsylvania, with her black Labrador Caley and her cat Josephine. When not in her studio, Rasmussen can usually be found somewhere in the garden or kayaking on the Delaware River.

# OTHER WORKS BY BEATRIX POTTER

*The Tale of Peter Rabbit* (1902)

*The Tale of Squirrel Nutkin* (1903)

*The Tailor of Gloucester* (1903)

*The Tale of Benjamin Bunny* (1904)

*The Tale of Two Bad Mice* (1904)

*The Tale of Mrs. Tiggy-Winkle* (1905)

*The Tale of the Pie and the Patty-Pan* (1905)

*The Tale of Mr. Jeremy Fisher* (1906)

*The Story of a Fierce Bad Rabbit* (1906)

*The Story of Miss Moppet* (1906)

*The Tale of Tom Kitten* (1907)

*The Tale of Jemima Puddle-Duck* (1908)

*The Tale of Samuel Whiskers or, The Roly-Poly Pudding* (1908)

*The Tale of the Flopsy Bunnies* (1909)

*The Tale of Ginger and Pickles* (1909)

*The Tale of Mrs. Tittlemouse* (1910)

*The Tale of Timmy Tiptoes* (1911)

*The Tale of Mr. Tod* (1912)

*The Tale of Pigling Bland* (1913)

*Appley Dapply's Nursery Rhymes* (1917)

*The Tale of Johnny Town-Mouse* (1918)